The Pigman

by Paul Zindel

Lit Link
Grades 7-8

Written by Keith Whittington
Revised by Ruth Solski
Illustrated by On The Mark Press

On The Mark Press
15 Dairy Avenue
Napanee, Ontario
K7R 1M4
www.onthemarkpress.com

OTM-14179 ISBN: 9781550355600

1

© On The Mark Press

At A Glance

Learning Expectations	Chapter 1	Chapter 2	Chapter 3	Chapter 4	Chapter 5	Follow-Up Activities Section 1	Chapter 6	Chapter 7	Chapter 8	Chapter 9	Chapter 10	Follow-Up Activities Section 2	Chapter 11	Chapter 12	Chapter 13	Chapter 14	Chapter 15	Follow-Up Activities Section 3
Reading Comprehension																		
• Identify and describe story elements	•	•	•	•	•		•	•	•	•	•		•	•	•	•	•	
• Locating the main idea	•	•	•	•	•		•	•	•	•	•		•	•	•	•	•	
• Recalling events and details	•	•	•	•	•		•	•	•	•	•		•	•	•	•	•	
Reasoning and Critical Thinking Skills																		
• Identify character traits	•	•	•	•	•		•	•	•	•	•		•	•	•	•	•	
• Contribute to character attribute webs	•	•	•	•	•		•	•	•	•	•		•	•	•	•	•	
• Make inferences (why events occurred, characters thoughts and feelings)	•	•	•	•	•		•	•	•	•	•		•	•	•	•	•	
• Develop opinions and personal interpretations	•	•	•	•	•		•	•	•	•	•		•	•	•	•	•	
Vocabulary Development, Grammar & Word Usage																		
• Recognizes types of nouns					•													
• Proper Usage of nouns					•													
• Synonyms/Meanings												•						
• Recognizing types of pronouns												•						
• Proper usage of pronouns												•						
Creative Writing																		
• Expresses ideas in complete sentences	•	•	•	•	•		•	•	•	•	•		•	•	•	•	•	•
• Making a sociogram																		•
Research																		
• Finding and documenting proof of a topic																		•

OTM-14179 ISBN: 9781550355600

The Pigman

By Paul Zindel

Table of Contents

The Pigman

By Paul Zindel

Objectives

- To acquaint the student with the writings of Paul Zindel
- To appreciate and enjoy the humor of Paul Zindel and to see his concern for wayward teenagers.
- To be able to see how other teenagers try to cope through the adolescent years and to be able to learn from their experience.
- To provide students with helpful resources which will enable them to make the right decisions about drinking and smoking during their teenage years.
- To promote creative, divergent, honest, oral and written responses.
- To practice a variety of comprehension skills.
- To create a Character Web and a Sociogram which are useful in the Novel Study Program.
- To provide a variety of "Challenge Activities" to strengthen the "creative mind."

Summary of Story

John Conlan is a sophomore, teenaged boy who hates school. He has done everything from bulding and setting off bombs in the boys' washroom to rolling apples along the floors in classrooms. Lorraine Jensen, a sophomore, is very quiet and has little, if any, self-confidence. John and Lorraine seemed to have bonded together looking for help from each other. Both teens were loners with no one to love and neither had any friends.

The local teenagers often gathered together to make the usual random calls to the elderly people of the community to have fun at the older peoples' expense. After making several calls, Lorraine happened to convince a lonely old man by the name of Pignati that she was collecting money for the L. and J. Charity Fund. Being preoccupied by the fact that someone was actually talking to him, Mr. Pignati forgot about the purpose of the call. He began to share himself in conversation about his vacationing wife and about his joke: the best get-well cards on the market.

Eventually, Mr. Pignati is talked into donating ten dollars to Lorraine's "charity." John is excited because now he can buy his six-pack of beer. Lorraine doesn't believe that this is right, but John points out that the old man needs visitors. "So it's our duty to visit the lonely."

As the story unfolds, the reader meets Lorraine's mother and John's two parents. Contact with John's and Lorraine's home life is continued throughout the story. It becomes quite evident why these two teenagers think and behave the way they do. All the reader needs to do is total up the personality traits of these parents and the sums are their respective children.

The Pigman

By Paul Zindel

When John and Lorraine meet Mr. Pignati, they notice his big beer stomach, twinkling eyes, and great smile. He welcomes John and Lorraine with open arms, asks them to sit down and have some wine.

In no time at all, a deep friendship is built up with the old man. They get a tour of the big house. He makes a point of showing them the "pig" room. Here his wife has collected hundreds and hundreds of pig figurines from all over the wolrd. They are of various colors, made of clay, plastic and glass. Mr. Pignati felt his wife deserved a pig when they had first met, to remind her of his name, Pignati. This room was very sacred and special to him.

The most important outdoor activity the three friends do together is to visit the primates and mammals at the zoo. The Pigman (Mr. Pignati) had made a special friendship with a baboon called Bobo. As days passed, John and Lorraine made it known to the Pigman that they were not truthful about the charity. After hearing this, the Pigman confesses that he too lied about his wife, Conchetta. She had died and he was still in mourning. He is alone but is now excited about his new friendship with John and Lorraine.

The Pigman's friendship and home life have become so much a part of John and Lorraine that they looked to him for security. The two were treated like family members with gifts such as rollerblades. One night, after walking to the zoo and shoveling snow, the Pigman had a heart attack while he was chasing John and Lorraine around the house. The teenagers called the ambulance and the Pigman was taken to the hospital.

John and Lorraine are entrusted with the care of the house while the Pigman recuperates from his attack. It is at this time John decides it would be "cool" to have a party of school teenagers at the Pigman's house. John believes the Pigman would have wanted them to have friends over for a small party.

Unfortunately, the party gets out of hand and the police are called. Besides noise, some damage was also done to the house. Norton Kelly, a demented acquaintance of John, came to the party uninvited and went on a rampage through the Pigman's house. In a rage of anger for not being invited, he totally destroyed the sacred room of pigs. John, besides being drunk, started fighting with Norton

As the reader might guess, Mr. Pignati had been released early by the hospital and arrived at his house shortly before the police came to break up the party. Besides not being very happy about what had happened, he was devastated when he saw the pig room. John and Lorraine were taken to their respective homes by the police. Their parents were not too happy as described by the author. Luckily the old man did not press charges.

The next day, John and Lorraine wanted to apologize to the Pigman and clean up the house. A telephone call was made by the two, but it took a lot of talking before the old man accepted the

apology. John proposed that the three go that afternoon to visit Bobo, the baboon, at the zoo. The old man gave in and agreed to go.

After an unusually long wait for the Pigman at the zoo, the three made their way through the gates. The Pigman was still very weak from his heart attack and extremely hurt and disappointed about the incident the night before. John, Lorraine and the Pigman tried to find their friend Bobo and the other baboons in the cage, but they could not be found. Quickly John asked one of the zoo's groundskeepers where Bobo was. He said that Bobo died of pneumonia the week before.

After hearing this the Pigman was struck with total grief so badly that for awhile he could not speak and his body began to tremble. In short time, he was able to give out a small cry and then collapsed. His heart gave way and he died. John and Lorraine are devastated by the loss of their dear friend.

John and Lorraine decide to write an epic memorial in honor of their special friend.

Author Biography

Paul Zindel was born May 15, 1963, in Staten Island, New York. He graduated from Wagner College with a B. S. in 1958 and a M. Sc. in 1959. He taught chemistry at Tottenville High School, Staten Island, New York, from 1959 to 1969. In 1969, he became a playwright and an author of children's books. He took his playwright-in-residence in Alley Theatre, Houston, Texas, in 1967. He is a member of Actor Studios. In 1973 he married Bonnie Hildebrand, a screenwriter. They have two children, David Jack and Elizabeth Claire.

Paul Zindel's early plays provided some excellent roles for actresses, but presently Paul's writings revolve around men's roles. He has commented, "Whatever I do becomes summarized in my writings. When I have gained a certain quantity of experience which begins to shape into something secret and interesting, I feel I must tell others about it." When he was asked if he was always a playwright, Zindel answered, "The fact I had written plays by the age of twenty makes me believe that the seeds of theatre are born inside us."

Paul Zindel received a Ford Foundation grant in 1967, for his The Effects of Gamma Rays on Man-in-the-Moon Marigolds. He won the Obie Award in 1970, the Pulitzer Prize in 1971, New York Critics Award in 1971, and the Vernon Rice Drama Desk Award in 1971. He received an honorary doctorate of humanities from Wagner College in 1971.

Paul Zindel's writings include:

- **Books at the Juvenile Level:**
  The Pigman
  My Darling, My Hamburger

OTM-14179 ISBN: 9781550355600

6

The Pigman

By Paul Zindel

I Never Loved Your Mind
Pardon Me, You're Stepping On My Eyeball
I Love My Mother
Confessions of a Teenage Baboon
The Pigman and Me
Pigman's Legacy
The Gadget
Rats
The Doom Stone
Fifth Grade Safari

- **Plays:**

Dimensions of Peacock
Euthanasia and Endless Hearts
A Dream of Swallows
The Effects of Gamma Rays on Man-in-the-Moon Marigolds
Ladies at the Alamo
Let Me Hear You Whisper

- **Screen and Television:**

The Effects of Gamma Rays on Man-in-the-Moon Marigolds
Let Me Hear You Whisper
The Pigman
Farewell to a Mouse Named Mars

Tips for Teachers

1. It is highly suggested that the classroom teacher has read this novel and additional materials before trying to implement this unit. Success depends on it!

2. This book is not intended to be used in its entirety. It is only a resource to accompany the novel study process. A teacher's background knowledge and enthusiasm are also important ingredients for success.

3. Lessons must be taught and guidance be given to students regarding Character Webs and the Sociogram of Characters.

4. Resource materials for Smoking and Alcoholism should accompany the program as I feel that Mr. Paul Zindel would have wanted the students to know about these choices at this time of their life.

The Pigman

By Paul Zindel

5. Teachers' answers for the Character Attribute Web, Sociogram for the Pigman, and Cause and Effect for John and Lorraine should not be considered absolute. They have been set up for the teacher as a guide only. The teacher is welcome to alter as she or he wishes.

Using a Character Attribute Web in the Novel Study Approach

1. Attribute Webs are simply a visual representation of a character from a novel. They provide a systematic way for the reader to organize and recap the information that he or she may have collected about a particular character.

   Attribute Webs may be put together after reading the novel to recapitulate information about a particular character or completed gradually as information unfolds. (It is much easier if done gradually.)

   This activity can be done individually or in small groups. (Check for instructions.)

2. Suggested questions used to help locate information.

   a) How does a character (John, Lorraine, etc.) act or feel in this certain situation?
      How would you feel if it happened to you?
      How do you think the character feels?

   b) How a character looks. Close your eyes and picture the character. Describe him or her to me

   c) Where a character lives: where? when?

   d) How the other characters feel or react regarding the specific character in question.

3. Collecting Data Tool: Skim carefully through the pages of each chapter locating information regarding the facts. Place it on the Attribute Web (Page 9). Use small phrases of words stating the fact. Be sure to record the page number where the information was found.

The Pigman

By Paul Zindel

Character Attribute Web

Does

_____
_____
_____
_____
_____
_____
_____
_____
_____
_____

Others' Actions

_____
_____
_____
_____
_____
_____
_____
_____
_____
_____

Says

_____
_____
_____
_____
_____
_____

Others' Say

_____
_____
_____
_____
_____
_____

Feels

_____
_____
_____
_____

Lives

_____
_____
_____
_____

Looks

_____
_____
_____
_____

OTM-14179 ISBN: 9781550355600

The Pigman

By Paul Zindel

Name: _____

The Pigman

By Paul Zindel

Section 1   **Chapter One Questions**

Vocabulary: porcelain avocation commemorative excruciating raunchiest

Answer each question with a complete sentence.

1. List three activities that John enjoyed doing in his early years at high school.

_____

_____

_____

2. Was John "taking responsibility for his own education?" Explain fully.

_____

_____

_____

3. Find four to six examples of humor that the author uses to point out facts about the story and to encourage us to read on.

_____

_____

_____

_____

4. Write five words or word phrases to describe the kind of guy John is.

_____

_____

_____

_____

_____

Attribute Web:
Begin to add information about our characters to the attribute webs as outline by your teacher. Record page numbers where each fact is found.

The Pigman

By Paul Zindel

Section 1:   **Chapter Two Questions**

Vocabulary: subliminally, thrombosis, infantile, homosapiens, abominable, mortified

Answer each questions with a complete sentence.

1. John and Lorraine decide to write this "memorial epic" now, instead of later. Give reasons why the epic will be important to the reader as well as to the writers themselves (see pages 6 and 15).

_____
_____
_____
_____
_____
_____

2. Show two ways the author points out to the reader the dangers of smoking.

_____
_____
_____
_____
_____
_____

3. Explain Lorraine's comment, "I think he used to distort things physically and now he does it verbally" (page7).

_____
_____
_____
_____
_____
_____

Attribute Web:

Continue to record facts. Remember to record pages as well.

The Pigman

By Paul Zindel

Section 1:   **Chapter Two Questions**

4. What is the meaning of the word "compassion?"

_____

Why doesn't John want to show compassion?

_____

_____

_____

_____

5. If you, like Lorraine, moved into a new neighborhood and enrolled at the high school, what kinds of difficulties in adjusting would you have? Explain fully.

_____

_____

_____

_____

_____

6. What does Lorraine mean by the "source problem" (page 7,10) when she is talking about John?

_____

_____

_____

_____

_____

7. What do you learn about both Lorraine and John from the meeting at "the bus scene?"

_____

_____

_____

_____

_____

Attribute Web:

Continue to record facts. Remember to record page numbers too.

The Pigman
By Paul Zindel

Section 1:   **Chapter Three Questions**

Vocabulary: amoeba, paranoia, fanatic

Answer each questions with a complete sentence.

1. John said that the Pigman was not "behind the times." What quality did he like about the Pigman?

   _____

   _____

   _____

2. What does John feel would help young Lorraine most of all?

   _____

   _____

   _____

3. Describe the two telephone activities in which John, Lorraine, and their friends had become involved.

   _____

   _____

   _____

   _____

   What are your feelings about these types of activities?

   _____

   _____

   _____

   _____

4. List several examples of humor the author has written in this chapter. Which example do you think is the funniest?

   _____

   _____

   _____

   _____

Attribute Web:

    Continue to record facts. Remember to record page numbers as well.

The Pigman

By Paul Zindel

Section 1:   **Chapter Four Questions**

Vocabulary: quivery, prevarication, syndrome schizophrenic

Answer each question in a complete sentence.

1. When Lorraine telephoned Mr. Pignati, what did she feel she had learned about him?

_____

_____

_____

_____

_____

2. John is a victim of the "compensation syndrome." Explain what you think it does for John.

_____

_____

_____

_____

_____

3. Find another example of "source problem" regarding John and the way he is.

_____

_____

_____

_____

_____

_____

Attribute Web:

Continue to add to your attitute webs.

The Pigman

By Paul Zindel

Section 1:   **Chapter Four Questions**

4. "Biting her lip" (page 30, 31), John is able to sway or bend Lorraine into doing what he wants to do. Have you ever been encouraged or "talked into" doing something that you felt was wrong or unfair? How did you handle it? Any difficulties?

_____

_____

_____

_____

_____

_____

_____

_____

_____

_____

_____

_____

5. Humor continues to build! List as many humorous parts of this chapter as you can.

_____

_____

_____

_____

_____

_____

_____

_____

_____

_____

_____

_____

_____

Attribute Web:

Continue to add to your attribute webs. Remember to put page numbers as well.

The Pigman

By Paul Zindel

Section 1: **Chapter Five Questions**

Vocabulary: demented, subsidize, attaché case, juvenile delinquent, hypertension, disdain

Answer each question with a complete sentence.

1. Lorraine says, "(John) pretends he doesn't care about anything in the world,... and real hostility he has..." (page 9). Find a comment by John that supports this (page 26).

   _____

   _____

   _____

   _____

   _____

2. John's family life doesn't seem to be very close and happy for all (page 27 to 28). Give two or three suggestions to John and/or his parents for improvement in the situation.

   _____

   _____

   _____

   _____

   _____

   _____

3. The author reminds us again of the dangers of tobacco and smoking. How is this done?

   _____

   _____

   _____

   _____

Attribute Web:

   Continue to add information and page numbers to your attribute webs.

The Pigman

By Paul Zindel

Follow-Up Activities for Section One

Part A: Nouns

A noun is a word which names a _____, _____, _____,
idea or feelings. There are different kinds of nouns.

1. *Common Noun:* A person, place or _____ the word is not _____.

2. Search through pages 1 to 3 (Chapter 1) and list examples for each type on the chart below.

Person	Place	Thing

3. *Proper Nouns:* A specific person, place or thing that is spelled with a capital letter.

Search the pages 1 to 3 of the novel and list examples of each type of proper noun.

Person	Place	Thing

The Pigman

By Paul Zindel

4. *Collective Nouns:* A single word that names a group or collection of persons, places or things.

    Examples:

jury	crowd	sheep	fish	police

5. A noun may be *singular* (one thing) or *plural* (more than one thing) in form. To form the plural of a noun, you usually add "s" or "es" to the end of the singular form.

    Examples:

rat - rats	book - books	peach - peaches	class - classes	box - boxes

    For some nouns, you will need to change letters when forming plurals.

    Examples:

wolf - wolves	goose - geese	baby - babies	woman - women

6. Searching through pages 1 to 39 (chapters 1 to 5), locate examples of plural nouns. The word found can be the singular or the plural noun, but you must present both the singular and plural of that noun. Record the page number where the word was located.

    Look for all three types.

"s" or "es"	Changing the Letters	Collective Nouns

OTM-14179 ISBN: 9781550355600

The Pigman

By Paul Zindel

Part B: Nouns

A. Underline the nouns in the following sentences.

1. I'd forgotten I had lit the bomb and it exploded.

2. Did you ever hear a herd of buffalo stampeding on the plains.

3. He always went to the Moravian Cemetery to drink beer.

4. She runs around like a chicken with her head cut off.

5. Cigarettes and alcohol are not good for your health.

B. Place appropriate nouns on the blanks in the sentences.
Choose your words from the following list. Use a word only once.

home	time	smile	donation	wine
charity	trees	animals	glasses	dogs
clouds	mother	wife	pamphlet	smoking

1. He returned with three _____ of _____ and that enormous _____ of his.

2. My _____ and I both love _____.

3. You wanted a _____, did you say, for what _____?

4. I was interested in looking at the _____ and _____ and stray _____.

5. Another _____ I forgot my _____ to bring _____ a _____ about _____.

The Pigman

By Paul Zindel

Section 2:   **Chapter Six Questions**

> **Vocabulary:** psychiatrist, psychoanalysis, antagonist, nocturnal room

Answer each question with a complete sentence.

1. Do you agree with Lorraine that Tony of Tony's Market isn't the best father image for youth? Explain.

_____

_____

_____

2. Lorraine doesn't appear to agree with John when it comes to drinking beer, smoking cigarettes and cashing the check. Why then does she stay with him? Explain.

_____

_____

_____

3. Read pages 41 to 44. Think about Lorraine's home life. Does she also have a "source problem?" Explain.

_____

_____

_____

_____

4. Why doesn't Lorraine enjoy visiting the zoo?

_____

_____

_____

5. Lorraine had uncomfortable feelings about bad omens. List the omens she had.

_____

_____

_____

_____

The Pigman

By Paul Zindel

Section 2: **Chapter Six Questions**

7. Find words or word phrases that describe Mr. Pignati's friend Bobo.

_____ _____ _____

_____ _____ _____

_____ _____ _____

_____ _____ _____

8. Travel through the zoo with the Pigman and unscramble the names of the animals you will see. Don't use your novel.

sinoi _____   teotr _____   dpelaor _____

eayhn _____   hetaech _____   rgiet _____

ophpis _____   lblu _____   netratea _____

9. John, Lorraine, and the Pigman are all acting like chimpanzees. What do you think the other people nearby are thinking about their actions? Explain

_____

_____

_____

_____

_____

10. Point out the most humorous part in this chapter. Explain why.

_____

_____

_____

_____

_____

_____

_____

Attribute Web:

Continue to record facts and record pages on your attribute webs.

The Pigman

By Paul Zindel

Section 2: **Chapter Seven Questions**

> **Vocabulary:** subliminal, voluptuous, perpetual, elaborate, hemoglobin, oscilloscope, floundering

Answer each question with a complete sentence.

1. Why does John find it necessary to use cursing or "street language" when he talks to people or refers to some idea?

   _____

   _____

   _____

   _____

2. Could this be a sign of maturity (growing up) by some people or all people? Explain.

   _____

   _____

   _____

   _____

   _____

3. John and his friends feel that the cemetery is a great place to be alone, to drink beer, and to scare people. Do you think that this is the "mature thing" to do when young people begin to become adults of the community? Explain your answer.

   _____

   _____

   _____

   _____

   _____

   _____

The Pigman

By Paul Zindel

Section 2:   **Chapter Seven Questions**

4. Why do the local communities have to spend so much money to repair the vandalism committed in the local cemeteries?

_____

_____

_____

_____

_____

5. John mentions that he and his friends go to the cemetery at midnight. That would probably mean that he and his friends wouldn't be home until three or four o'clock in the morning. Do you spend late hours like this through the week? Explain.

_____

_____

_____

_____

_____

6. What are your thoughts about "curfews" (a municipal law stating at what time young people ages twelve to eighteen must be off the street and in their family homes)? Explain

_____

_____

_____

_____

_____

7. List some facts from the story that proves John does worry about death and life ever after. Record the page number where the facts were found.

_____

_____

_____

_____

_____

The Pigman

By Paul Zindel

8. Is it good that John's father continually points out to John how great his brother Kenny is? Comment.

_____

_____

_____

9. Has this happened to you before (with a brother or sister)? Discuss your feelings about it.

_____

_____

_____

_____

10. What does John see for his brother and his father if both continue to work at the Exchange?

_____

_____

_____

_____

11. What is it that John tells his dad he wants most in life?

_____

_____

_____

12. A great friendship has been built among the three people - John, Lorraine, and the Pigman. Copy the sections that prove this to be true.

_____

_____

_____

Attribute Web:

Continue to build up the attribute webs on the novel's characters.

The Pigman

By Paul Zindel

Section 2:   **Chapter Eight Questions**

> **Vocabulary:** encyclopedias, tragedy, escalator, ricotta cheese, arsenal, suspicious, delicatessen

Answer each question with a complete sentence.

1. Why do you think it was so hard for the Pigman to talk about his wife's death?

    _____
    _____
    _____

2. Lorraine thinks love between a man and a woman is the strongest thing in the world. Can you agree with Lorraine? Express your thoughts about this.

    _____
    _____
    _____

3. Homeless people (some of whom are alcoholic) are also found in small cities and towns. What can you do at your age to help these kind of people? Explain

    _____
    _____
    _____

4. Why did John and Lorraine let the Pigman spoil them in the Beekman's Department store?

    _____
    _____

    Was this appropriate behavior for the two teenagers?

    _____
    _____
    _____

Attribute Web:
    Continue to record facts and their page numbers on the attribute webs for each character.

The Pigman

By Paul Zindel

Section 2:   **Chapter Nine Questions**

Vocabulary: Cro Magnon man, berserk, putrid, sclerosis

Answer each question with a complete sentence.

1. Norton suggests that he might want to break into Mr. Pignati's house and steal "whatever." Why didn't John try to talk him out of it?

   _____

   _____

   _____

   _____

   _____

2. Why was it so easy for John to take to drinking with his friends?

   _____

   _____

   _____

   _____

   _____

3. The Pigman had become such a big contrast to John's own parents and he liked this. Explain.

   _____

   _____

   _____

   _____

   _____

   _____

   _____

   _____

Attribute Web:

Continue to record facts and page numbers on your character attribute webs.

 # The Pigman

By Paul Zindel

> **Vocabulary:** interrogating, mooching

Answer each question with a complete sentence.

1. Describe how John and Lorraine felt when they decided to tell the Pigman about the charity check. How was this good for the Pigman to hear?

   _____
   _____
   _____

2. What did the three friends do to show how important each one was to the other?

   _____
   _____
   _____

3. The Pigman tells a "murder story" to John and Lorraine. Did it really point out some truth about their preference of these qualities?

   _____
   _____
   _____

4. Are activities such as the Pigman's game, reading horoscopes in the daily newspaper, going to fortune tellers, and telephoning 1-900 psychics helpful in shaping your behavior and future? Explain.

   _____
   _____
   _____

5. Point out the most humorous part in the chapter. Tell why.

   _____
   _____
   _____

Attribute Web:
   Remember to add facts and page numbers to the character attribute webs

The Pigman

By Paul Zindel

Follow-Up Activities for Section Two

Part A: A Visit to the Zoo

Find and mark only the false facts by putting a check mark in the blank following each statement.

Baboons

1. They carry food in pouches inside their cheeks. _____

2. Several kinds of baboons live only in Africa and southwestern Arabia. _____

3. It is the females that are the fighters and protectors of the group. _____

4. Hamadryas and Chacms are two groups of baboons. _____

5. Baboons' legs are shorter than their arms. _____

6. Baboons eat eggs, fruits, grass, insects, leaves, and roots. _____

7. Baboons are basically a large monkey without a tail. _____

8. A harem consists of three males, several females and young baboons. _____

Gnus

1. There are two kinds of gnu: brindled gnu and the white-tailed gnu. _____

2. A gnu eats insects, worms, and green beans. _____

3. These animals are found in Northern ireland and northern South America. _____

4. The gnu has thin legs and a horse-like tail. _____

5. This animal ranges from reddish-brown to gray in color. _____

6. The gnu is a large African antelope. _____

7. The white-tail gnu is almost extinct. _____

The Pigman

By Paul Zindel

Follow-Up Activities for Section Two

Part B: Synonyms

A synonym is a word or phrase that means the same (or almost the same) as another word.

For example: close - shut; lift - elevate

Using a dictionary or a thesaurus, find and write synonyms for the following words found in the novel "The Pigman."

1. voluptuous (page 34) _____

2. avocation (page 2) _____

3. perpetual (page 56) _____

4. prevarications (page 22) _____

5. hostility (page 9) _____

6. raunchiest (page 54) _____

7. putrid (page 82) _____

8. subliminal (page 54) _____

9. excruciatingly (page 5) _____

10. bellowed (page 22) _____

11. demented (page 26) _____

12. infantile (page 7) _____

13. abominable (page 9) _____

14. disdain (page 34) _____

The Pigman

By Paul Zindel

Follow-Up Activities for Section Two

Part C: Pronouns

- A *pronoun* is a word that takes the place of a noun.

  a) John hated school. He set off twenty-three bombs.

  b) The ghost of Aunt Ahra did housework. It was the cause of John's unrest at home.

  c) Friends are necessary for everyone. They like to share a party with us.

  To what or whom do the words he, it, they, and us refer?
  If you think about it, you'll see that he refers to John. Then you'll probably figure out that it refers to ghost, they refers to friends, and us refers to everyone.

  > The words to which pronouns refer or take the place of are called **antecedents**.

- There are different kinds of pronouns. The most commonly-used kind is the personal pronoun.

  > A **personal pronoun** can refer to one or more persons or things.

  a) Mr. Pignati always went to the zoo. He liked to visit Bobo.

  b) John and Lorraine were friends. They liked to play telephone games.

  c) The room was filled with pigs. It was very special to the Pigman.

1. Find and write five sentences or parts of sentences which use personal pronouns. Be sure that your choices illustrate the use of *person* and *thing personal pronouns*.

  _____

  _____

  _____

  _____

  _____

  _____

  _____

  _____

The Pigman

By Paul Zindel

Follow-Up Activities for Section Two

Part C: Pronouns

- Some personal pronouns show possession or ownership and act like adjectives. These pronouns are called possessive pronouns.

  For Example: Norton is your friend

  The pronoun "your" shows possession and therefore is a *possessive* pronoun.

  Other possessive pronouns are:

  | my   mine   yours   his   her   its   our   ours   their   theirs |

2. Fill in the blanks in the sentences below with the appropriate personal pronoun or possessive pronoun. Select these pronouns from the box above

   a) Lorraine's aunt bought _____ a book for Christmas.

   b) John and _____ friend packed _____ bags and left for the

      the country.

   c) Do _____ think Dennis can find _____ name in the book?

   d) Please save _____ for _____ verocious baboons.

   e) Norton saw _____ cheating at _____ card game.

3. **Circle** all pronouns and **underline** the nouns.

   a) Her white frilly dress was special to him.

   b) How do we know if they are able to come home?

   c) If you bring yours and I bring mine, then we'll have enough games for the party.

 # The Pigman

By Paul Zindel

Section 3: **Chapter Eleven Questions**

Vocabulary: bubonic plague, congealed

Answer each question with a complete sentence.

1. When the police came to take Mr. Pigman to the hospital, why did John and Lorraine give false information? What are your feelings about what they did?

_____

_____

_____

_____

_____

2. What favor was asked of John and Lorraine by the Pigman after they were leaving the hospital?

_____

_____

_____

_____

_____

_____

3. John and Lorraine had a special evening at the Pigman's house. List many of the special things about it.

_____

_____

_____

_____

_____

Attribute Web:

Continue to record facts and pages on the character attribute webs.

The Pigman

By Paul Zindel

Section 3: **Chapter Twelve Questions**

> **Vocabulary:** antifermenting

Answer each question with a complete sentence.

1. Since the special evening, what changes had Lorraine seen take place in John and what new feeling had she gotten about herself? Explain.

_____

_____

_____

2. On Friday, at the Pigman's house, John and Lorraine role-played a husband-wife relationship. What signs did you see that would destroy a happy, loving relationship? Explain.

_____

_____

_____

3. Who had taught John and Lorraine how to play these character roles?

_____

_____

_____

4. After cleaning the house, John told Lorraine it was time for a party and friends. Should he have made that decision himself? Explain.

_____

_____

_____

Attribute Web:

Continue to add information to the attribute webs.

The Pigman

By Paul Zindel

Section 3:　　　　　　　　**Chapter Thirteen Questions**

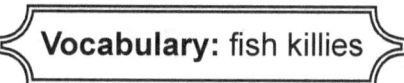

Vocabulary: fish killies

Answer each question with a complete sentence.

1. "They were a real bunch, but each of them had a problem of their own" (page 119). Make your own party list and invite your friends (three girls and three boys) to a party. Note: Use false names for your friends. List each name and a particular problem that you can see each person having. Set up a chart as shown.

Person	Problem	Behavior/Attribute
Helen	overweight	little confidence
Jane	very, very tall	self-conscious, upset, cries
1. _____	_____	_____
2. _____	_____	_____
3. _____	_____	_____
4. _____	_____	_____
5. _____	_____	_____
6. _____	_____	_____

2. Would you join this band of musicians after what you know about them? Explain.

_____

_____

_____

_____

3. John refused to stop the party while Lorraine still worried about the damage that had been done and the noise they were making. You are asked to do something. What do you do? Explain.

_____

_____

_____

The Pigman

By Paul Zindel

Section 3:   **Chapter Thirteen Questions**

4. How would you have handled Norton Kelly when he arrived uninvited to the party? Explain.

_____

_____

_____

5. What happened to the Pig Room?

_____

_____

_____

_____

6. Illustrate the scene in the Pig Room after the party.

Attribute Web:

Continue to build up facts on the Attribute Webs.

The Pigman

By Paul Zindel

Section 3:   **Chapter Fourteen Questions**

Vocabulary: incongruous, exaggerated, enthusiasm, proficiency, protruding, pneumonia

Answer each question with a complete sentence.

1. "...I hated John at that moment for having gotten me into this" (page 130). Is Lorraine taking responsibility for her earlier actions regarding what has happened? Explain.

_____

_____

_____

_____

_____

2. "We've seen you hanging around there before" (page 130). Discuss how important Neighborhood Watch Programs and regular police patrols are in our communities. How can you help?

_____

_____

_____

_____

_____

3. When the police brought Lorraine home, state four ways her mother reacted.

_____

_____

_____

_____

_____

The Pigman

By Paul Zindel

Section 3   **Chapter Fourteen Questions**

4. In these moments of frustration, what is it that Lorraine wanted to yell back to her mother but failed to do (page 132)?

_____

_____

_____

_____

_____

_____

5. Describe how John and Lorraine must have felt when they made the telephone call to Mr. Pignati the next morning.

_____

_____

_____

_____

_____

_____

_____

6. What did John suggest the three of them do that day?

_____

_____

_____

_____

_____

7. Was it a good idea for everyone?

_____

_____

_____

_____

Attribute Web:

Continue to contribute facts and page numbers on the Attribute Webs.

The Pigman

By Paul Zindel

Section 3:   **Chapter Fifteen Questions**

Answer each question in a complete sentence.

1. Why didn't Lorraine stay with John until the ambulance and police arrived?

_____
_____
_____
_____
_____

2. John pointed out something that he didn't like in this world of ours (a social illness). Discuss.

_____
_____
_____
_____
_____

3. What is John's greatest fear in life regarding how he is to shape his behavior, his attitude, and his role?

_____
_____
_____
_____
_____

4. John's belief for a useful and productive life is based on four influences. What are they?

_____
_____
_____

Attribute Web:

Continue to record facts and pages to each one.

The Pigman

By Paul Zindel

Follow-Up Activities for Section Three

Part A: Do parents and home life shape attitudes and behavior?

- Present day sayings:

> "The apple doesn't fall far from the tree."
>
> "He/She is a chip off the old block."

- It is said that we are often products of our home; therefore, let us find out if this is true when we consider John Conlan and Lorraine Jensen.

1. Use the collecting data tool for attribute webs in order to create a personal profile on each of the characters considered.

2. Proceed through each chapter carefully to collect all the facts and information. Be sure that each of the characters has his/her own attribute web.

3. It may be necessary to use more than one collecting tool for each character, for example John and Lorraine.

4. When facts for the fifteen chapters have been collected for the characters requested, then cause and effect must be considered.

5. You will need three copies of the page entitled Shaping Attributes and Behaviors - two for both John's parents and one for Lorraine's mother.

6. Select five or six dominant characteristics of each parent and show their effect on their respective child (John or Lorraine). All facts must be taken from the Character Attribute Webs and with the required page number (location found in the story).

7. Summarize your findings regarding parent dominant characteristics and state the resulting self-image for their child as per their influence as a parent.

The Pigman

By Paul Zindel

Shaping Attitudes and Behaviors

Effects of Parents and Home Life

Child's Name: _____

Cause ⟶	Effect
_____	_____
_____	_____
_____	_____
_____	_____
_____	_____
_____	_____
_____	_____
_____	_____
_____	_____
_____	_____

_____ Self-image ⟵

(Child's Name)

OTM-14179 ISBN: 9781550355600

The Pigman

By Paul Zindel

Follow-Up Activities for Section Three

Part B: Making a Sociogram for the Pigman

1. Place the names of the following characters in boxes below. Characters will include John, Mrs. Jensen, Mr. Conlan, Mr. Pignati, Lorraine, Mrs. Conlan, Dennis, and Norton

2. The characters should be arranged around the central characters. Place them in a suitable arrangement based on relationships.

3. Connect with lines or arrows. With brief statements, show directions and the nature of relationships

The Pigman

By Paul Zindel

Follow-Up Activities for Section Three

Part C: Cigarettes and Alcohol

1. See if John has made the wrong choice regarding smoking cigarettes. <u>Search</u> through the story. <u>Document</u> the phrases and the page numbers.

_____

_____

_____

_____

_____

_____

_____

_____

_____

_____

_____

_____

_____

_____

2. See if John has made the wrong choice regarding drinking alcohol. <u>Search</u> through the story. <u>Document</u> the phrases and page numbers.

_____

_____

_____

_____

_____

_____

_____

_____

_____

_____

The Pigman

By Paul Zindel

Follow-Up Activities for Section Three

Part D: Loneliness of the Elderly - A Concern

The school board has asked you and your class to set up a new program in your school. The program is called "Eliminating Social Problems in a North American Democracy."

The assignment is to design a program which will help eliminate loneliness of the aging adult.

1. Make a list of ideas of how you would go about linking up the students with the residents of the local retirement home(s) in your area.

2. Point out the benefits of this program to various members of your community.

3. Design and set up a classroom or an added building to the school (money is available) which will be needed to carry on with the program outlines by students and elderly.

4. Suggest various indoor and outdoor activities which would benefit both groups of people.

5. Create a slogan to encourage "work" to begin now.

6. Design a poster to advertise the program.

The Pigman

By Paul Zindel

Answer Key

Section 1 - Chapter Questions

Chapter One:

1. Bathroom bomber; supercolossal fruit roll; writing graffiti on desk/table tops.
2. Answers will vary.
3. Answers will vary.
4. Possible answers: risk taker; uses street language (cursing); has poor self-concept; likes to brag (23 bombs); needs attention from others
   Attribute Web: Discussions are important if pupils don't understand the process or are not finding all the facts needed.

Chapter Two:

1. If waited later:
   a) wouldn't have wanted for fear of embarrassment. To selves: would probably have forgotten much of it; give themselves time to look over and ask why they did crazy things.
   b) so readers can learn by their example; avoid wrong things/improve future for themselves and others
2. Lorraine points out dangers/case history S. Freud. Pamphlets/book from Lorraine (page 7)
3. Physically: things he did regarding question 1, chapter 1, smoking/drinking
   Verbally: cursing, manipulating other people to think like him. Answers will vary.
4. Compassion: kindness, empathy, grace for others; John doesn't want others to believe he is a wimp, soft - toughness is it! Answers will vary.
5. Answers will vary.
6. Source Problem: the beginning, where it all starts. For example: home, family, source of personal problems
7. Both brought out each other's need for a friend to recognize similarities in each other. Mostly similar problems that each have: poor self-concepts/little confidence, no friends and parent(s) who lack loving parenting skills. Answers will vary.
   Attribute Web: Discussions necessary during early chapters to verify if pupils understand process and are finding facts regarding personalities of characters.

Chapter Three:

1. The Pigman referred to John and Lorraine as "delighful", not cards, jazzy, cool or hip (page 14).
2. Lorraine needs a little confidence.
3. Telephone gags - for example: fridge running, telephone talking, marathon. Answers will vary.

The Pigman

By Paul Zindel

4. Dennis' hideous skin disease; description of Lorraine's mother; what John did on the telephone. Answers will vary.

Chapter Four:
1. Voice sounded excited; appeared to enjoy a joke; wanted to share one with Lorraine; Lorraine sensed a feeling of loneliness.
2. This process helps to give John's life some excitement. Telling lies not only becomes fun for John, but the lies become real forms of truth to him.
3. John's father is not only a braggart but cheats on insurance claims.
   Attribute Web: Reminder to pupils

Chapter Five:
1. "I didn't want anyone really to take advantage of the old man" (page 26).
2. Answers will vary.
3. Lorraine to John: "You're ruining your lungs with the thing..." (page 30).
   Attribute Web: Collecting data

Section 1: Follow-Up Activities:
Part A - Nouns
1. person, place, thing
2. thing, capitalized
3. person: guy, captain
   place: school, bathroom, class, floor
   thing: factors, smoke, bombs, firecrackers
   Answers will vary.
4. Information only.
5. Information only.
6. s: candle - candles (page 1); eyeball - eyeballs (page 12); eye - eyes (page 15); lock - locks (page 16)
   es: lunch - lunches (page 2); bench - benches (page 20)
   change word: shelf - shelves (page 38); fifty - fifties (page 31)
   collective nouns: of gestapo (page 2); of buffalo (page 3); old junk (page 32)

Part B - Activities
A. 1. bomb 2. herd, buffalo 3. Moravian Cemetery, beer 4. chicken, head
B. 1. glasses, wine, smile (page 33)
    2. wife, animals (page 37)
    3. donation, charity (page 24)
    4. trees, clouds, dogs (page 10)
    5. time, mother, home, pamphlet, smoking (page 7)

The Pigman

By Paul Zindel

Section 2 - Chapter Questions:

Chapter Six:
1. Answers will vary.
2. Answers will vary.
3. Answers will vary.
4. She wears dark glasses, doesn't like people looking at her, hates to see animals, birds and fish locked up for people to stare at (unkind), believes feeding animals should be game time. Remembers parent refused her a pet when she was young (but she does care about them). Answers will vary.
5. women selling peanuts, attacked by a peacock, a kid staring through glass at her
6. needs a spray deodorant, ugliest, monstrous teeth, most vicious looking
7. lions, otter, leopard, hyena, cheetah, tiger, hippos, bull, anteater
8. Answers will vary.
9. Answers will vary.

Chapter Seven:
1. Answers will vary.
2. Answers will vary.
3. Answers will vary.
4. Answers will vary.
5. Answers will vary.
6. Answers will vary.
7. "I was just interested in what was going to happen to me... something...more exciting than decaying" (page 56)
8. Answers will vary.
9. Answers will vary.
10. drop dead of heart attacks (page 58 to 59)
11. Wants to become an actor, to be individualistic, to be me, to give me time to find out who I am (page 58)
12. John and Lorraine: given a glass of wine, Mr. Pigman "shone" with happiness
    Mr. Pignati: wants to show John and Lorraine around the house, "Just make yourself at home!"

Chapter Eight:
1. Answers will vary.
2. Answers will vary.
3. Answers will vary.
4. Answers will vary.

Chapter Nine:
1. Answers will vary.
2. Answers will vary. "...why I'm the way I am" (page 84); Ten years of age, John would empty the beer glasses/bottles; Bore (John's father) thought it was great....; entertainment for him and his company; John liked it because he got attention from everyone.
3. Mr. Pigman's approach and relationship with John were good and warm. "John, please do whatever you like...feel at home...smile... he meant it" (page 85)

Chapter Ten:
1. Answers will vary. Hearing their lie about the charity check forced him to open up about the death of his wife.
2. "If one of us did something that...had to come up with...three copy cats" (page 93)
3. Answers will vary.
4. Answers will vary.
5. Answers will vary.

Section 2 - Follow-Up Activities

Part A - A Visit to the Zoo
Baboons
1. True
2. True
3. False - males are
4. True
5. False - arms are about as long as its legs
6. True
7. False - all types have a tail
8. False - only one male

Gnus
1. True
2. False - not worms and green beans
3. False - northern Kenya, northern South Africa
4. True
5. False - from brown to black
6. True
7. True

Part B - Synonyms
Answers will vary.
1. sensuous
2. hobby
3. eternal
4. trickery deceptions, sophism
5. feud, hatred
6. sexually, vulgar
7. rotten, corrupt
8. at sub-conscious level
9. intensively
10. roared

The Pigman

By Paul Zindel

11. insane
12. childish, immature
13. detestable, repulsive
14. ardent, eager, zealous
15. scorn, contempt

Part C - Pronouns

1. **Answers will vary.**
   Examples: ... I used to ignore it...; ... it didn't matter...; ...he is an actor...; ...you've heard of us...; ...we depend on lovely people...; I think he knew...

2. Answers will vary sometimes.
   a) her, him, them   b) his, their   c) you, his   d) it, them, his, her, their   e) her, them, him, his, her, their

3. a) (her) dress (him)   b) (we) they (home)   c) (you) (yours) (I) (mine) (we'll) game party

Section 3 - Chapter Questions

Chapter Eleven:

1. John was afraid of what Lorraine's mother would do to Lorraine. Lorraine was too scared to think clearly (page 100). Answers will vary.
2. Stop by the zoo, see and feed Bobo, tell him that Mr. Pigman misses him, take care of him, look after the house for me (page 104)
3. John dressed up in Pigman suit/moustache; Lorraine wore one of Conchetta's dresses; Lorraine cooked supper (spaghetti); candles on the dinner table; acted out lover scene and kissed

Chapter Twelve:

1. He wore shaving lotion, combed his hair (page 115), agreed to take out the garbage (page 112 to 113). When Lorraine thinks back to the candlelight evening, it was the first time that she was glad to be alive. She had a feeling something beautiful/wonderful would happen to her, but she would have to wait for it.
2. Answers will vary.
3. Answers will vary.
4. Answers will vary.

Chapter Thirteen:

1. Answer chart will vary. Good classroom discussion is needed.
2. Answers will vary.
3. Answers will vary.
4. Answers will vary.
5. Norton totally destroyed the room by smashing many of the pigs.

The Pigman

By Paul Zindel

Chapter Fourteen:

1. Answers will vary, but it sounds as if Lorraine is blaming John for the whole affair. I don't see her standing up for what she feels is right. Good class discussion regarding various responses is needed.
2. Answers will vary.
3. "Where are your clothes?" (twice) Slapped Lorraine's face (twice). Voice Level: hysterical to "commander". Started crying (appeared very hurt). Was it an act? (page 131). Lorraine's comment: once the stage is over...
4. "You really don't know me mother! I'm a human being also. I'm not a little girl anymore. I need to have friends besides you" (page 132).
5. Answers will vary.
6. "We could meet you at the zoo..." (page 137).
7. Answers will vary.

Chapter Fifteen:

1. John still feared for Lorraine's welfare regarding her mother's reaction.
2. "We live in a world where you can grow old and be alone and you have to get down on your knees to beg for friends" (page 144)
3. John would rather die than shape himself (behavior/attitude); role-taking into the kind of grown-ups that he is familiar with (his parents, Lorraine's parents and others like them) (page146).
4. God, death, universe, love

The Pigman

By Paul Zindel

Section 3 - Follow-Up Activities:

Part A - Shaping Attitudes and Behavior

Character's Name: John

Mother	John
Cause ———————▶	**Effect**
1. Complainer (page 27, 136, 85)	1. Complained about Lorraine's housekeeping and cooking (page 114)
2. Fanatic cleaner (page 27, 136, 85)	2. Fanatic about how he wanted breakfast (page 114)
3. Told John he aggravates his father (page 57).	3. He believes in his own lies (page 23).
4. She is a compulsive liar. (page 24,25).	4. "In the middle of everyday fantastic lies" (page 6).
5. Constantly telling John what to do, when to do it (page 136).	5. "...He (John) was always so infantile at home (page 6)
6. "Mother, your hypertension is showing" (page 29).	6. "I'm just as screwed up as he (Norton) is" (page 84).
7. She worried more about rinsing the glass than drinking the beer (page 85).	

John's Self-image ◀———————

• alcohol and smoking will kill him	• no independence	• picked on, no friends
• no trust	• all screwed up	• home disturbance

The Pigman

By Paul Zindel

Section 3 - Follow-Up Activities:

Part A - Shaping Attitudes and Behavior

Character's Name: John

Father	John
Cause ——————————————→	**Effect**
1. Compulsive alcoholic (page 10, 84) Encouraged John to drink at an early age	1. Developed excessive drinking of beer, wine (page 55, 117); at times was drunk (page 130, 55)
2. A great liar (page 24, 25)	2. Everyday told a fantastic lie (page 6, 7, 23, 24)
3. Ridiculed John constantly (page 60, 58); said John had too much spare time (page 59)	3. John is maladjusted at times (page 114); got elected Bathroom Bomber (page 1)
4. believed John needed a psychiatrist (page 135)	4. I'm just as screwed up as he (Norton) is. (page 84)

John's Self-image

←——————————

• alcoholic like father

• a disturbing influence at home

• no friends

The Pigman

By Paul Zindel

Part A - Shaping Attitudes and Behavior

Character's Name: Lorraine

Mother	Lorraine
Cause ➡	**Effect**
1. Constant ridicule from mother about her appearance, ie. hair, dress, and the way she walked (page 7,9,15), said Lorraine was too fat (page 9)	1. "I'm not a pretty girl" (page 9), she remembers the words (page 15)
2. She believed all men are sex maniacs (page 31).	2. Lorraine made comment about the Pigman "or he could be a sex maniac" (page 31).
3. Mother slapped Lorraine's face several times (Page 132).	3. "her (mother's) eyes burned into me" (page 131); most of all I had paranoia (page 11).
4. Mother is a very pretty woman who hardly smiles (page 43).	4. "...if you ask me, all she needs is a little confidence" (page 15)
5. "(Mother) needs three years of intensive psychoanalysis (page 42), "... her problems are so deep rooted" (page 42).	5. John called her "a little schizo" (page 41).

Lorraine's Self-image ⬅

- no self-confidence
- no friends

- fear of parent
- house cleaning lady

OTM-14179 ISBN: 9781550355600

The Pigman

By Paul Zindel

Section 3 Follow-up Activities

Part B - Sociogram

Example of a set-up with brief statements

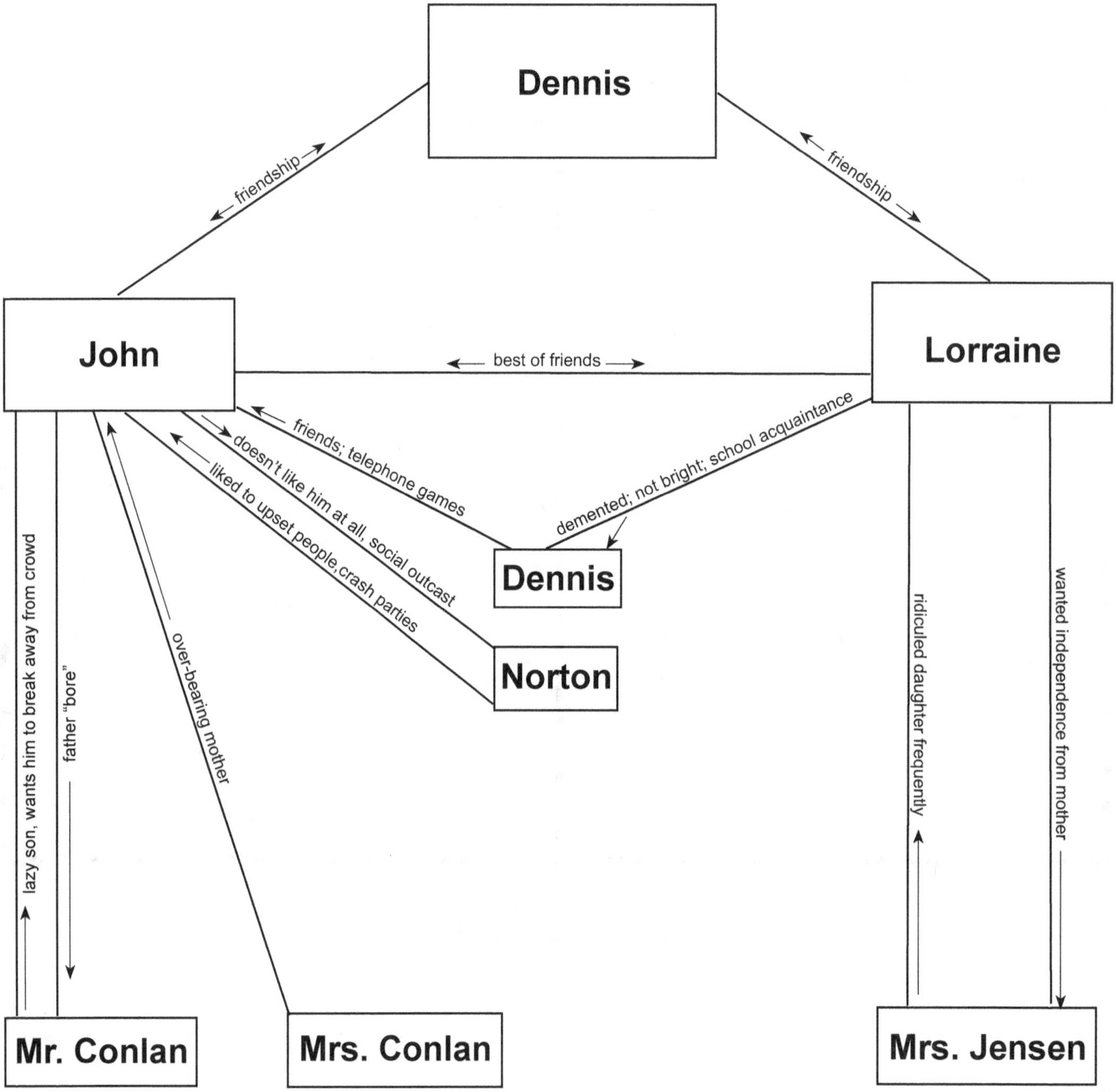

Dennis

friendship →
← *friendship*

John

← *best of friends* →

Lorraine

← *friends; telephone games*

← *doesn't like him at all, social outcast*

← *liked to upset people, crash parties*

demented; not bright; school acquaintance ↓

Dennis

Norton

lazy son, wants him to break away from crowd

father "bore"

over-bearing mother

ridiculed daughter frequently

wanted independence from mother

Mr. Conlan

Mrs. Conlan

Mrs. Jensen

The Pigman

By Paul Zindel

Section 3 Follow-Up Activities

Part C - Cigarettes and Alcohol

1. I tried to explain to him how dangerous it was (page 7). I got my mother to bring home a pamphlet about smoking (page 7). I could hear Lorraine's voice saying I was killing myself. As if I didn't know it! I knew what it was doing to me (page 146). Because he wanted a pack of cigarettes (136).

2. He always went to the Moravian Cemetery to drink beer (page 7). I just stared at him drinking beer (page 40). Norton invited me to the cemetery to have a beer (page 82). I took a sip of beer (page 83). He (Bore) got a big kick out of it... about ten years old... emptying all the beer glasses (page 84). John breaking down and buying his own six-packs of beer (page 89). I told him to steal a bottle of 80-proofer out of his father's whisky cabinet (page 118). He (John) was hopelessly drunk (page 131).

Part D - Loneliness of the Elderly

Suggested Steps Taken by the Teacher:
1. Teacher, principal, and community leaders for elderley activities discuss the need for student/school contact with seniors in the community.
2. Teacher outlines aims/objectives for the program "Bridging the Gap - Students and Seniors."
3. Look at three approaches:
   a) Seniors in own homes.
   b) Seniors in retirement homes who can get to drop-in centers.
   c) Seniors in nursing homes unable to leave.

Student Involvement:
1. Able to work around homes:
   a) wash windows; trim trees, bushes, garden; paint outside of house/fence; wash cars
   b) run errands, shopping
   c) spend time with people
2. Allow half-day once or twice per month to come to retirement home:
   a) play cards, board games
   b) do crafts such as learning to quilt, needle work on pillow cases and dish towels
   c) students put on a small play, have a sing-song, entertainment
3. Volunteer in other ways:
   a) help deliver meals, assist with feeding (something like candy-stripers in hospitals)
   b) help write letters for seniors; read to them; converse with them

Getting Started:
1. Teacher and students discuss need for such a program; then set aims and objectives. Students, teacher and principal search for volunteers to help with supervision needed to

ensure students work through activities/chores.

2. Advertise in local newspapers, posters, radio. Meet with the mayor. promote a special day or week for "Bridging the Gap." Possible television coverage.
3. Students have a telephone survey and knock on doors of seniors to seek work to be done.
4. Any money given to students for work done is to be given to senior activities in the community.
5. Close contact with leaders and co-workers within the elderly facilities.

Benefits for Students and Seniors:
1. Self esteem
2. awareness of seniors'/students' interests, knowledge
3. new worthwhile relationships
4. good feeling of team effort
5. awareness of their own future needs
6. gaining new skills: social, educational, physical

The Pigman

By Paul Zindel

Attibute Webs

Character Attribute Web

Does

makes bombs re: bathroom;
supercolossal fruit roll; write on desks;
curses, drinks, smokes; gets drunk in the
cemeteries; likes to make homeless
people tell life stories, watch their
embarrassment; complains to Lorraine
about her housekeeping/cooking.

Others' Actions

_____
_____
_____
_____
_____
_____
_____

Says

John #1

Others Say

hates school, everyone curses, I am
very handsome, fabulous eyes, I
remember the action; feels being
picked on/not trusted by father;
compassionate, visits the lonely;
thinks of becoming an actor; I
want to be me.

extremely handsome; has a family no one
would believe; usually isn't telling the
truth; has compassion deep inside him; has
fantastic eyes; hates Norton; believes he
tells lies to mother/father; he'll end up
complicating things; isn't afraid to wear
silly things

Feels

Lives

Looks

felt scared when he arrived at
Pignati's house for money;
cemeteries loveliest places
to be; wants to do something
after death; believes father will
die from strain of work; wants
to be himself.

_____
_____
_____
_____
_____

The Pigman

By Paul Zindel

Attribute Webs

Character Attribute Web

Does

slipped a lit cigarette into the hand of a dummy; young, would empty beer glasses; cut school class to visit Mr. Pignati in hospital; punched Norton and felt good about it; in middle of everyday fantastic lies

Others' Actions

_____
_____
_____
_____
_____
_____
_____

Says

I really do hate Norton; would kill Norton if he harmed the old man; told Dennis to steal 80 proofer from his dad; Mr. Pignati "we feel terrible about the party"; "I'm just as screwed up as he is."

John #2

Others Say

when young, Bore would say "Johnny wants a sip of beer"; kid will be a great drinker; John turn radio down, John you're disturbing your father, etc.; saw John's infantile behavior in Pigman's house; John is maladjusted at times.

Feels

felt at times just as screwed up with life as Norton was; had become a distrubing influence at home; really felt Mr. Pignati wanted them to have a few friends over; mother and father never really loved each other.

Lives

_____
_____
_____
_____
_____
_____

Looks

The Pigman

By Paul Zindel

Attribute Webs

Character Attribute Web

Does

didn't want to take money from Pignati; doesn't like wearing crazy clothes; fell asleep at night crying thinking about the things her mother said about her; lies about her name to the police; lies to saleslady (I'm his niece); lies to her mother about where she was.

Others' Actions

_____
_____
_____
_____
_____
_____
_____
_____

Says

I'm not exactly the most beautiful girl in the world; first two weeks of moving no one spoke to me; says animals should play a game to get food; told Mr. Pignati they would miss him.

Lorraine #1

Others Say

your hair would be better cut short; you're putting on too much weight; you wear clothes funny; she remembers the words' needs a little confidence; has interesting green eyes; wants to be a writer; easily swayed by John; was sad when they met Pignati; has a gift for saying things that make you feel anxious; John called her a little schizo; sounds just like her mother when she says that.

Feels

believes she has a family no one would believe (make her sick); she has paranoia; if she had been able to have a dog when younger, would have been great; felt so sad for Pigman alone.

Lives

_____
_____
_____
_____
_____
_____

Looks

The Pigman

By Paul Zindel

Attribute Webs

Character Attribute Web

Does

cut school with John to visit Mr. Pignati; has a nightmare about Pignati's house; lies to her mother where she is phoning from; cried thinking about the destroyed Pig Room

Others' Actions

mother slapped her twice across the face; tried third time also

Says

let me be a child, my mother would never let me be one; felt embarrassed because she found herself begging in front of the police (afraid of her mother); "or he (Mr. Pignati) could be a sex maniac."

Lorraine #2

Others Say

mother complained about her effort to bake cake, "horrible" taste, waste of money; constant warning about getting into cars; she looked beautiful dressed up; constantly asking her to do do housework/skip school; "that sounds like her mother again."

Feels

I began to get terrified at what my mother would say; couldn't make up her mind about the Pigman buying articles for her and John; mother hated father for what he had done.

Lives

_____
_____
_____
_____
_____
_____

Looks

The Pigman

By Paul Zindel

Attribute Webs

Character Attribute Web

Does

_____
_____
_____
_____
_____
_____

Others' Actions

_____
_____
_____
_____
_____
_____
_____

Says

Mr. Donlan

(John's father)

Others Say

John has too much spare time; calls John a jackass; tells him to work; wants John to stands out in his own way, individualistic; get his hair cut; you look like an oddball John.

was a compulsive alcoholic; set a bad example for John's early age (sign of father's immaturity); frightened of John's lies; does not have an imagination; just as bad when it comes to lying; braggard, phoney insurance; did have sclerosis of the liver; he looked sick and old; quit drinking

Feels

Lives

Looks

felt John should go to a psychiatrist

_____
_____
_____
_____
_____

The Pigman

By Paul Zindel

Attribute Webs

Character Attribute Web

Does

shines coffee table; plastic covers on everything; worried about snow, stairs.

Others' Actions

_____
_____
_____
_____
_____

Says

rinse out the glass; complains about John eating peas; brags about her husband

Mrs. Donlan (John's mother)

Others Say

is a disinfectant fanatic; plastic covers; frightened about John's lies; doesn't have a great imagination; just as bad when it comes to lying; lies about Green Stamps; hypertension is showing' "they're just as bad as he is when it comes to lying

Feels

believes John aggravates his father

Lives

_____
_____
_____
_____
_____

Looks

The Pigman

By Paul Zindel

Attribute Webs

Character Attribute Web

Does

is a nurse; steal goods from patients; takes money for favors; slapped Lorraine across the face twice; acted out, crying

Others' Actions

_____
_____
_____
_____
_____

Says

her eyes burned into me; Lorraine not most beautiful; boys only have one thing on their minds; borrowed goods from another (steals); complains about not having any nylons; takes money on the side (favors); says Lorraine could miss school; will steal cleanser from work; housework to be done by Lorraine

Mrs. Jensen

(Lorraine's mother)

Others Say

she distorts things; believes all men are sex maniacs; she is enough to worry about; is a very pretty woman, hardly ever smiles; sounds different than she looks; needs three years of intensive psychoanalysis; all her patients felt to be sex maniacs; she did pick on me now; I knew her mother would have shipped her to Tibetan convent.

Feels

says lock all doors and windows; don't answer door bells; complained about Lorraine's skirt too short; concerned about Lorraine's clothes.

Lives

_____
_____
_____
_____
_____

Looks

The Pigman

By Paul Zindel

OTM-14179 ISBN: 9781550355600